TEMPT the DEVIL

Tempt the Devil

A prequel novella

Savage Hearts Empire

Kimberly Quinn

The characters and events in this book are fictitious. Any similarity to real persons, living or dead, is coincidental and not intended by the author.

Editing: Happily Editing Anns

Cover Design: Marika Veil

978-1-989112-37-3 (ebook)

978-1-989112-38-0 (paperback)

Wanting her breaks the rules. Taking her rewrites them.

Róisín Glynn is here to steal from my enemy. It's my job to make sure she's on task. Or take her off the board.

But she isn't supposed to look like temptation. She isn't supposed to move like she owns the room. Or lie with a voice that makes me want to hear her beg.

She's clever. Controlled. Braver than she should be. And completely unprepared for the kind of attention she's just triggered. Because mine is the kind that marks. Stalks. Claims.

She's playing a part to survive. But I'm playing to own every move she makes. And I never lose.

Especially when she wants to be caught.

Content Warning

This book contains dark and adult themes which may be triggering for some readers. These include but are not limited to:

- Abduction (off page and unconfirmed)
- Alcohol use
- Profanity
- Physical violence
- On page sexual acts, including acts of Voyeurism and BDSM, including breath play
- Murder
- Criminal acts, including theft

For the introverts.

Chapter 1

Róisín

Even with a gun to my head, I wouldn't call this a smart plan.

But I'm here anyway. Dressed to seduce, armed with a lie, and about to execute the most dangerous hack I've ever attempted.

In person.

"This is insane," the blonde ahead of me squeals to her friend, her voice slicing through my thoughts. "It's so freaking glamorous."

The rope drops, and I'm ushered into the elite club behind them. Like I belong. Like this place isn't notorious for being impossible to get into.

Just another Friday night, folks. Nothing to see here.

"Very *Gatsby*," the other woman says, flicking her hot-pink hair over her shoulder as she bounces on her toes, already high on anticipation.

They're here for the thrill. For drinks, dancing, and drama. Maybe a little debauchery.

Not me.

I'm here to clean up someone else's mess. To cross a line I hope doesn't end with me buried six feet under. Because I don't have a choice.

If I did, this scheme sure as hell wouldn't involve me dressed as bait.

A bouncer stands inside the entrance, his featureless black mask giving off a sort of serial-killer vibe. It's super charming. Especially when he gives us a slow once-over, like he's mentally noting which of us might scream the loudest.

Without a word, he steps aside, and just like that, I'm past the point of no return.

My skin prickles, and I get the sense his eyes aren't the only ones tracking me. But I keep my pace steady, posture straight, and pray the gold filigree covering the upper half of my face hides what I'm thinking.

Because the giddy blonde has one thing right—this really is insane.

"Let's get drinks." She loops her arm through her friend's and flashes me a bright grin. "Want to join us for some fun?"

Right. *Fun.*

Probably not a bad idea if I want to blend in.

I nod, giving her what's meant to be a smile but feels more like a grimace, and trail after them to the bar.

The club swallows us in a haze of heat, glitter, and sound. Soft, warm light spills from massive gold fixtures above, catching on crystal glassware and metallic accents. Velvet-draped booths line the walls. Gilded mirrors reflect flashes of movement and skin. The polished marble floor makes my choice of three-inch heels feel not only questionable but downright dangerous.

The Black Crown is nothing like a normal nightclub. At least, not the kind I'm used to, with sticky floors, strobe lights, and half-conscious strangers grinding to bad remixes over spilled vodka coolers.

Everything here reeks of money. Luxury. Power.

And sex.

Champagne flows like water. Laughter cuts through the music as though orchestrated. Expensive perfume hangs in the air.

And everywhere I look, people are dancing, drinking, whispering to one another. All of them masked like me.

The mask O'Shea's men gave me came in a plain black box. No note. No explanation.

Only expectation.

Despite everything it represents, I've got to admit, it's beautiful.

Gold filigree curls across my cheekbones in delicate spirals, rising over my forehead in a pattern of twisted thorns and vines. A red satin ribbon holds it in place, and a red gem dangles beneath one eye like a single bloodstained tear. It's elegant. Dramatic. Eye-catching.

The opposite of everything I've ever been.

With it on, I almost feel like someone else. Someone bolder, fearless, and seductive. The kind of woman who not only fits in but can stand out in this world, instead of hiding behind a computer screen.

But the mask isn't a disguise. It's a directive.

Because I'm not a guest, and despite appearances, I'm not here to have fun.

I'm a pawn. A strategically placed asset, expected to perform. Dropped into the lion's den to retrieve what O'Shea wants most. And if I don't deliver...

Fuck, I can't let myself think about it.

The guns. The threats. How good his men are at making people and problems disappear.

Not when my brothers are both gone because of them—Grady to prison, Garrett to the grave—and I'm all that's left. The only one standing between my grieving father and the goddamn mob.

Grady owes them a debt. Like it or not, this is how it gets paid.

One night. One job.

Slip into the club. Get close to Bowen Alexander, a billionaire CEO with shiny political ambitions and dirty connections. Skim the data from his phone using the custom tool stitched into the lining of my clutch.

No questions. No mistakes.

And they didn't need to say *or else* for me to understand there's no backing out.

At the bar, the blonde orders dirty martinis for us without asking, then spins to face me with the easy confidence of someone who's never second-guessed a decision in her life. "Figured we should match the vibe. I'm Liv, by the way, and this is Kayla."

Kayla wiggles her fingers with a smile. "Glad you decided to stick with us. Nights like this are way more fun with a group."

"I'm Robin." The fake name tumbles from my lips like I was born with it.

And in a way, I was. It's the name stamped across my work badge, courtesy of an HR error no one ever bothered to fix, despite a year's worth of emails. The same name I used as a joke online and somehow ended up building an entire persona around. A fabricated identity I've hidden behind more often than I care to admit.

At this point, *Robin* gets more action than I do.

Liv grins. "Nice to meet you, Robin. What do you do when you're not wandering into clubs with strangers?"

"Cybersecurity." I grab for the drink the bartender sets in front of me. "I'm a penetration tester."

They both stare, waiting for the punch line.

"An ethical hacker," I explain, even though I hate that title, because apparently tech-speak isn't hot in heels. "I help companies test their security by trying to break it."

Kayla lets out a laugh. "Shit, did you hack the guest list? Is that how we all got in?"

I smirk, even as my stomach sinks. "What can I say? IT never sleeps."

They laugh like it's just banter. Like I'm someone fun and harmless, out for nothing more than a good time.

But that's not me. At least, not tonight, when everything I

care about is riding on what happens next. And not when Kayla's joke hits a little too close to the truth.

The martini's salty bite slides down my throat, and I let the burn settle in my stomach, calming my nerves as I scan the crowd.

A blur of half-hidden faces moves around me. Bodies press close. Masks catch the light. But there's no sign of Bowen Alexander.

Of course not. That would be too easy.

If the intel's right, he's rarely in the open. Too high profile to mingle, he prefers a private booth. One where he can watch the room, choose who's worth his time, and summon them at his convenience.

I stand like static in a room full of signal, attempting to blend in while my new friends chatter about the elegance on display. I smile and nod at whatever Liv just said. Pretend I'm still with them. Still present. And try to ignore the flicker of attention scraping across my skin.

It's subtle, but insistent. A signal that pings, vanishes, and pings again. Like something tracking me in the background, waiting for a response.

I take another sip of my drink, still scanning.

Then freeze.

A man stands near the edge of the dance floor, cloaked in shadows like the light knows better than to touch him. He's tall, broad, and maddeningly composed, watching the room with the kind of ease that says he's not here to impress anyone. He doesn't need to be part of the scene to command it.

And holy hell, can he fill out a suit.

Black, tailored, and clinging in all the right ways, it accentuates the solid muscle beneath. It makes him look dangerous. Menacing.

Or maybe that's the effect of his mask.

It conceals everything but his jaw and mouth, shadowing his eyes, draping him in just enough mystery to be infuriating. But it's the horns that do it. They curve up over the top of his head, making him look like something wicked. Like he moonlights as the devil himself.

And he's watching me.

No. He's staring. As if I'm the most fascinating thing he's seen all night.

My breath catches, stomach drops, and a spark flashes up my spine.

Who the hell is he?

And why do I have the sudden urge to find out?

Chapter 2

Keir

She's not what I expected. Nothing like the timid mouse I was told she'd be.

There's fear in her, sure. But it's coiled tight beneath the surface, held firm by something bolder. Sharper.

Defiance, maybe. Or the rush of getting away with shite she knows she damn well shouldn't.

She's no pro, that's clear enough. But she's not some wide-eyed innocent, either. No, she's more than a good Irish girl dragged into the muck by her feckless older brothers.

The little rose is pure control.

Quiet. Intense. Fucking disarming.

And yeah, she's the job. But that's not why I can't take my eyes off her.

It's the way she walked in with her head high, arse wrapped in that sinful red dress, daring anyone to come at her. Expecting danger. Looking for a taste like she's hungry for it.

Doesn't hurt that she's fucking stunning.

With all that wild auburn hair, legs that'd look perfect around my waist, and curves made to ruin a man, she's fucking irresistible. More temptation than I've faced in a long, long time.

Her friends, whoever the hell they are, don't hold a candle.

They're all flash and noise—the blonde begging for trouble, and the pink-haired one reeking of desperation.

But Róisín Glynn?

She's something else. A trap dressed up like a goddamn treasure.

Composed. Calculated. Every move holds a secret. Every glance is a warning. She's dangerous in ways that have nothing to do with the job she's here to pull.

And she knows I'm watching.

She holds my stare like she recognizes exactly what I am. Knows every dirty thing I've done. Can see the blood on my hands and the bodies I've left behind. And still doesn't give a shite.

Not about the danger. Or the consequences.

As if she's just daring me to try and claim her.

A deep hunger claws its way through me. More than a passing attraction or simple curiosity, this is raw, feral fucking need. The kind of craving that gets under your skin and stays there.

The kind that makes a man forget the plan.

All I can think about is cracking her composure. Pushing her over the edge of that carefully guarded control and making her come undone beneath me.

Will she break loudly? Softly? Will she fucking beg?

My uncle gave me a simple job—watch her, stay out of sight, and clean up if things go wrong. Take her out if it comes to that.

But that order was handed down by a middleman. As if I was just another one of his lackeys. No explanation. No trust. Just a demand for loyalty from the untouchable Gael O'Shea.

A test. Even though I've never failed him.

Tonight will be no different. He'll get what he wants. I'll do my part and make sure Róisín plays hers.

But from a distance?

Not a fucking chance.

Chapter 3

Róisín

He's still watching me. Still setting my skin ablaze like it's his favorite hobby.

The corner of his mouth crooks. He knows he's been caught and feels no shame. Hell, he likes that I'm looking. Probably expected it.

But I have no idea who this stranger is.

Unflinching and intense, his gaze pins me in place. It's as though he can see all my poorly constructed lies and wants to unravel every single one.

With his teeth.

My pulse hammers and I hold his stare a little too long. Because apparently, I have no sense of self-preservation.

Desire pulses to life between my thighs. The ache is sharp and demanding, burning through me with unrelenting ferocity.

He's dangerous. That much is obvious.

But I can't make myself look away.

There's something magnetic about him. Something that, despite the whole brooding shadow-demon aesthetic, makes me want to cross the room and ask his name. To see what happens next. To find out how far this attraction goes.

Fuck, I want nothing more than to get lost in it. To get out of my head, out of the script that's been written for me, away from the duty that's got me trapped, and let my body lead for once.

To be someone else for the night. To become the bold, daring woman I'm currently cosplaying.

But movement in my periphery breaks the spell, reminding me why I'm here.

And it's not to get caught up with a sexy-as-sin stranger.

I tear my gaze away, drag in a shaky breath, and focus on the mission. On the small group of men cutting across the floor. Most importantly, the one in the center.

He's in a sleek suit and expensive-looking mask, with his silver hair perfectly styled. Every detail is engineered to project power. But it's the way he moves that confirms it. He has the lazy confidence of someone who's always been in charge—wealthy, worshipped, and untouchable.

Bowen Alexander.

Corporate kingpin. Aspiring political golden boy. The man with a polished public image and corrupt private empire. The one that mob boss Gael O'Shea wants cracked wide open.

His entourage matches the profile. Four men, all clearly muscle. They're alert, and running perimeter while pretending to blend in.

Bowen doesn't bother looking. He radiates entitlement like the night exists just for him. Like he owns the damn building and everyone in it.

Hell, maybe he does. It wouldn't shock me to find out he charges a premium for the air we're all breathing.

The martini glass trembles in my hand, and I risk a glance at Liv and Kayla, half expecting them to notice. But they're still laughing, talking. Completely unaware that I'm on the verge of passing out or puking.

I tighten my grip and breathe through the rush of adrenaline.

This is it.

Everything I've been told, everything I've planned—none of it feels like enough now that the program is running live. No more simulations. No undo key. This is real.

And it's happening now.

My breath draws short as I track Bowen through the crowd. He stops near a red velvet curtain at the far wall, says something to the man beside him, then disappears behind it without a backward glance. Three of the men follow, leaving one to stand guard outside.

The man left behind positions himself in front of the curtain, his shoulders squared and gaze sharp. A human firewall.

Well, fuck.

"What the hell," Liv mutters, pulling my focus. "Where are they going?"

"Who?" I ask, trying to sound casual.

"The guy in the fancy suit with the security detail." She nods toward the other side of the room. "They just vanished behind that curtain."

Kayla squints. "Maybe it's a secret VIP lounge or something?"

"No idea,"—Liv downs the last gulp of her drink and sets the empty glass on the bar—"but there's only one way to find out."

Before either of us can react, she's gone, slipping into the crowd and heading straight for the draped velvet like it's calling her name.

"She's not actually..." Kayla says, sounding stunned.

But of course, she is.

Honestly, I don't know why Kayla's surprised. We've just met, but it's already clear Liv's the type who follows chaos around like it owes her money. Or worse, she creates it.

My gaze drops to my half-finished drink. The air feels too thick, and my pulse won't settle. I'm not ready.

But fuck, will I ever be?

I drain the rest of the martini in two swallows and set the glass beside Liv's.

The look Kayla gives me is curious, maybe a little wary. "Are we actually doing this?"

"I don't think we have a choice." At least, I don't.

If Bowen Alexander is behind that curtain, so is my mission. My one shot at dragging my family out of the mess my brother got us tangled in.

And I didn't squeeze myself into this dress just to watch it slip away.

By the time we move from the bar, Liv's already across the room. She stops at the curtain, spins on her heel, and flashes us a giant grin like she's won a dare.

"Unbelievable," Kayla mutters beside me as we push through the crowd to catch up.

I can't help but agree—Liv is reckless. But she's also handed me the perfect excuse to follow Bowen.

"Took you long enough," Liv chirps as we finally reach her.

Kayla rolls her eyes. "Well, we're here now..."

"Then what are we waiting for?" Turning, Liv threads her arms through ours and tugs us forward. "Let's find out what's hiding behind curtain number one."

I nod, Kayla sighs, and Liv steers us straight toward the guard.

He greets us with a smug grin, his shoulders shaking with barely contained laughter like we're the comedic fucking highlight of his night.

Screw him.

Screw all these criminal-minded men who think power excuses everything. Who destroy lives without losing sleep over it. I might be caught in the middle of whatever power play or dick-measuring contest this is, but that doesn't mean I have to take crap from this overpaid doorman.

I shove back the fear trying to crawl up my throat and step forward. "We're going in there."

"Be my guest." His mouth twitches, and he lifts the curtain, gesturing us through.

No password. No clearance check. Just an invite to ruin.

Without a second thought, I take it.

I step through first, but Liv and Kayla slip ahead of me as the heavy fabric falls closed behind us.

The music dulls to a distant thud. The air grows thick. Overhead, the lights cut out, except for the harsh glow of a single hanging bulb.

This doesn't feel like a nightclub anymore. More like the start of an interrogation fantasy. Or the opening of a horror movie come to life.

Fuck, this is such a bad idea. There's no way I can outrun a killer in these heels.

The hallway veers hard left, and another overhead bulb buzzes to life, guiding the way.

Panic hums beneath my skin, sharp and electric, but I keep moving despite it. Turning back now isn't an option. That's how systems fail—hesitation, lag, glitches that turn fatal.

Another light flares to life ahead, just as the one behind us dies. The ornate black-and-gold wallpaper shifts with every step, making it feel like the walls are alive. Watching. Closing in.

It's disorienting. Disturbing. As though we've slipped out of the main program and into a hidden subroutine. A back door only accessible by invitation. Or mistake.

But maybe that's the point. This is a test, and only the bravest make it through.

Or it's a trap. A rabbit hole lined in velvet and bad decisions.

Either way, it's too late.

My only choice is to fall.

Chapter 4

Róisín

Another masked bouncer waits in the shadows at the end of the darkened hallway. He tilts his head as we approach, nodding toward a door.

Silent and waiting. Creepy as hell.

What are we supposed to do—give a password? A bribe? A blood sample?

It would've been nice if someone from O'Shea's crew had mentioned this part—given me a warning or at least a heads-up. Anything.

Instead, I'm walking in blind, completely out of my element and trying not to show it.

Liv doesn't even blink. She strides forward like she's done this a hundred times, and the bouncer opens the door with a theatrical bow. It's so over-the-top, I half expect him to break into song.

She walks in. Kayla follows.

And when I step through, I almost crash into both of them.

"What the hell?" I mutter, squeezing between them. But stop cold.

A spotlight cuts through the dark haze, illuminating the center of the room and making everything around it seem to fade away. And in that circle of light...

Sex.

Actual sex. Live and unfiltered.

Bodies are on full display. Chains, whips, and leather masks are used as props. Hands grope. Mouths seek. Flesh slaps against flesh with fervor.

It's graphic. Indulgent.

And, if I'm being honest, way more intriguing than it has any right to be.

The door clicks shut behind us, trapping me in the dark with two near strangers, an orgy, and a to-do list from the mob.

I blink hard, dragging my gaze from the spotlight and the writhing bodies, and force myself to look around.

Focus. Adapt. Don't drool.

Low tables, chairs, and divans are scattered across the floor like seductive traps, each one artfully positioned to encourage regrettable choices. At the far end, a gold-drenched bar gleams beneath the soft glow of amber sconces.

The same red velvet booths as the front room curve around small tables, each framed by heavy red-and-gold curtains. Most are open, offering a perfect view of the show. A few are drawn shut, concealing whatever's going on inside.

I'm really not sure I want to know.

The booths line a raised section several steps up from the main floor.

Because of course there's a VIP area. Bouncer included. He stands at the bottom of the short staircase, guarding the elite from the rest of us lowly sex fiends.

Above it all, the ceiling stretches high, but somehow the space still feels closed in. Intimate.

The kind of intimate that demands you strip something before you're welcomed—your inhibitions, your judgment, your clothes.

"This place just keeps getting better and better," Liv cries, clapping her hands like we've stumbled into an upscale cabaret instead of a porn palace.

"You match the room," Kayla whispers in my ear.

She's right. The entire space is draped in crimson and gold. Just like my mask and the dress that wasn't designed for breathing.

And I can't shake the feeling it's not a coincidence.

My pulse spikes.

Fuck, I shouldn't be here. Not like this—exposed and unarmed, with only a hack stitched into my clutch and nerves barely held together by faulty logic and lies.

Liv strides deeper into the room, practically vibrating. Kayla drifts after her, seemingly mesmerized by the naked strangers fucking only feet away as if it were performance art.

I make myself move. One step, then another.

My fingers mold tight around my clutch as I scan the room, searching for silver hair. A security detail. A man who acts like the world belongs to him.

Where the fuck is Bowen Alexander?

A waitress drifts past in sheer black lace, a tray in one hand and a collar tight around her neck. She sees us but keeps walking. No offer of drinks. No greeting. Not even a judgmental sneer.

She knows we don't belong.

That truth sinks deeper the closer we get to the center of the room, tightening around my chest.

We're interlopers here. Noise in the system.

And we're being watched.

The feeling slithers through me, setting my nerves on edge. But I do my best to ignore it and continue searching.

Until my eyes land on him. The man in the devil mask.

He moves through the room with purpose, unfazed by the scene playing out under the spotlight. Or the loud moan that echoes through the space. His gaze locks on me like he never lost track.

Like he's a predator and I'm the prey.

And unfortunately, my body likes that idea. A lot.

My pulse hammers, thighs clench, and electricity shoots up

my spine. All at once, I'm too hot and flustered. Too goddamn turned on.

I square my shoulders, forcing my gaze away before I melt to the floor or launch myself in his direction. Honestly, either's possible at this moment. And I cannot afford to deviate from the plan. Not now. Not for a man in a mask who wears danger like a religion.

I need to find Bowen, get what I came for, and get the hell out.

"Come on." Liv grabs Kayla's hand, steering her toward the nearest open seats.

Perfect.

If they're busy entertaining themselves, they won't ask questions. Hell, they might not even notice if I disappear entirely. Especially if there's another act to this floor show.

I hang back a few steps, scanning again. Only, slower this time.

Finally, I spot the man I'm here for.

Bowen Alexander lounges in a sleek, high-backed chair in the VIP section like he's posing for his villain origin photo. Shadows and yes-men flank him, and the curtains around his area are tied back as if it's a stage set just for him.

He's showing off. Daring someone, anyone, to approach him.

Fuck, there's no way I'm getting a private audience. Which might be a good thing, since there's probably not a way out for me that doesn't involve a body bag.

But I don't need a meeting. Only proximity.

A few days ago, I sent him a spoofed press app, pitched as a digital questionnaire from a major news outlet. It was glossy and flattering, designed to feed his ego and slip past his firewall in one click.

According to my tracker, he opened it. Which means the embedded payload should still be sitting dormant, waiting to sync the second I get within range. If his phone's connected to the club's Wi-Fi—and let's be honest, someone like Bowen probably insists on five bars of signal everywhere he goes—the device in my clutch will handle the rest.

Six feet. That's all I need.

If I can get close, linger a moment, and let the tech do its thing, it'll be like stealing candy from a megalomaniac.

I glance at Liv and Kayla. They've sunk into their chairs, making themselves at home.

"I'm going to grab another drink." I motion toward the bar.

Kayla glances over, giving me a dazzling smile and thumbs-up. Liv doesn't even look. She's too busy watching the kink on display.

And just like that, it seems my brief girl-gang era has come to a close. It's probably for the best. We were always on borrowed time.

Still, there's something about them—wild, bright, and alive. The kind of energy I don't let myself touch too often. It might've been nice to hold on to it a little longer. God knows my social circle could use some expanding. Right now, it's all coworkers, usernames, and the baristas who enable my caffeine addiction.

But tonight's mess and the risk I'm being forced to take? It's mine. And I'm not about to drag Liv and Kayla any deeper into it.

Chin up, tits out, I put a little extra swing in my hips and move toward the VIP area like I'm just another rich girl enjoying the party.

The bouncer watches as I approach. His featureless black mask is the same as the one at the front door, which means I have no clue what he's thinking.

Am I fooling him? Who the hell knows.

My legs shake, but I keep moving, each step landing harder than the last.

Twelve feet.

Nine.

Seven.

Almost there.

But I hit the base of the stairs and there's still no signal from the device.

Bowen's phone is out of reach. My only hope of making this work is to get closer. There's no choice. I've got to get up there.

But the bouncer blocks me with an outstretched arm. "Members only."

I flash what I hope passes for a seductive smile. "Can't you make an exception? Just this once?"

Before he can answer, a man jogs down the steps, calling for us to wait.

Shit. It's one of Bowen's men.

He leans in and whispers something to the bouncer, then turns and grabs my arm. And he's not nice about it.

"Excuse me." My voice is sharp, despite the jolt of fear rushing through me.

But he doesn't let go. Even the bouncer has stepped aside, unbothered by the fact I'm being touched without permission.

What happened to consent? Isn't it supposed to be the golden rule in a place like this?

The guard drags me up the stairs, grip like a vise. "Mr. Alexander has invited you to join him," he says, as though it excuses his behavior.

"He could've just asked."

"He doesn't need to," he says through a cruel laugh. "Don't pretend it's not what you wanted."

He's not wrong. Getting close to Bowen was the objective. But how many women has he hauled up these stairs in this same way—willing or not?

Does the entitled asshole ever not get what he wants?

Fear slams through me as we hit the landing, and my step falters the minute I see Bowen seated in his throne of self-importance. There's nowhere to hide. No way to run.

So, I lift my chin again, paste on a smile, and do what I came here to do.

Play the part.
And pray I make it out in one piece.

Chapter 5

Keir

Róisín's not the show, but she's got my full, undivided attention, regardless.

Not even the naked woman getting plowed at center stage—bent at the waist, legs spread wide, and body gleaming under the lights—can distract me.

A paddle cracks across skin. The crowd flinches. The woman moans loud enough to rattle the fucking rafters.

All of it's a show. Performed and packaged for the room. Designed to shock and entertain the voyeurs.

Salacious, sure. Taboo, maybe.

But it's the fakest shite I've ever seen.

Róisín, though?

She's the real fucking deal. Every glorious goddamn inch of her.

Even done up in fuck-me heels, that deadly red dress, and lips painted to tempt the devil, there's nothing overdone about her. She doesn't strut or play coy.

She doesn't need to. Without lifting a finger, she owns the room and every man in it.

And underneath all that beauty? The sweet little rose has thorns.

Even from this distance, I can see the bite beneath her blush. She's sharp enough to steal a man's heart. After she's cut it straight out of his chest.

And Christ, I want to be the one bleeding.

I don't know her. Not truly. But it doesn't matter.

Tonight, she's mine.

There's a dark flicker of pride twisting in my gut as she moves in on the target—graceful, confident, and fucking devastating. Every sway of her hips dares the world to come closer. Her arse rolls like a challenge, attracting looks whether she means to or not.

It's enough to make a lesser man forget his own name.

She reaches the base of the members-only balcony, and the bouncer blocks her path. Still, she doesn't lose her composure.

Until real trouble steps in. One of Bowen's lapdogs.

His hand clamps around her arm like he's staking a claim. Marking her as the property of Bowen Alexander.

The prick doesn't know it yet, but he just signed his own death warrant with that move.

Róisín doesn't wilt, though. Not one bit.

She snaps back, all bite and fire, and even though I can't make out the words, I'd bet my last bullet they weren't polite. Still, it doesn't stop the little shite from dragging her up the stairs.

My jaw locks. Fists curl tight. Veins burn with the urge to break something—preferably his fucking head.

I know the plan.

She needs to get close to Bowen. It's the whole bloody reason we're here, and the only way the theft works, if I understand it right.

But this?

Standing by while his hired help—some smug little prick with a borrowed ego and running on borrowed time—puts his hands on her? Watching her get marched up the stairs like a gift-wrapped whore to the sleaziest bastard in the room?

Fuck no.

My uncle might not give a shite. To him, she's a pawn. Disposable and replaceable.

But I'm not playing by those rules. Not when she's already proven she's got more backbone, more grit, and more bloody value than half the lads he's keeping on payroll.

And not when I've got the means to stop it.

My gaze drills into the thick bastard dragging her along. He yanks her closer, sneers at her attempt to get free, and laughs as she stumbles.

And I start counting all the ways I'm going to make him bleed.

Chapter 6

Róisín

"You look lost." Bowen's tone is flat, his expression bored.

If his welcome was any warmer, I might catch frostbite.

But I don't trust his aloofness. I get the distinct feeling he's baiting me. Waiting to pounce.

And there's still no signal from the device.

Fuck, I'm in so much trouble.

"Lost? Why would you think that?" My voice dips low as I ease closer, despite every instinct screaming at me to back away. "You invited me. At least, that's what your man said."

"I did." His mouth cracks into a practiced, charming smile that makes my stomach turn.

Still, I take another step forward.

"And you accepted," he says, as if I sent an RSVP instead of being practically abducted. "You must know who I am."

"Of course. I know exactly who you are." *Power-drunk egomaniac.*

A sharp buzz hits my palm, and I let out an anxious breath. Finally, I've achieved sync.

Thank fuck.

The data pull has started. Now all I have to do is not die before the upload finishes.

But I'm boxed in. Trapped between the man who dragged me up the stairs—twice my size and still lingering too close—and the arrogant threat of Bowen Alexander.

And let's not forget the other two guards who flank him. They're watching me like they're already planning how to clean up my blood once their boss is done with me.

Sixty seconds. That's all I need. One minute to grab the data and disappear.

Assuming I can figure out how the hell to do that.

Bowen tips his head. "Why don't you come sit?" His voice is still flat but there's a glint in his eye that makes my skin crawl.

I glance around, confirming what I already know. There's only one chair in the space. And he's sitting in it.

His unsettling smile widens as he motions to his lap.

Oh, hell no.

"Thanks, but I'd rather stand." I keep my tone nice and neutral, even as revulsion claws at my throat.

His demeanor shifts. The smile he's wearing doesn't slip. His gaze doesn't waver. But his amusement fades, replaced by something cold and hostile.

It's a look that sends my heart racing. And not in the fun, flirty kind of way.

"You're not nearly as stupid as you look." His words are cruel, meant to offend, but I'm too scared to be insulted. "Which means, you're not here by accident."

My polite smile stretches thin. "I was just curious. This is my first time at the club, and it's all so glamorous. Then I saw you and—"

"Bullshit." His harsh tone cuts me off. "You're a reporter, aren't you?"

"What?" *Fuck, fuck, fuck.* "No, I'm not. I swear."

"No?" he taunts. "If that's true, I'm sure you won't mind if we check."

My instincts scream at me to run, but before I can get my legs to work, Bowen lifts a finger.

Instantly, a familiar, punishing grip clamps around my arm again, and I look up to find my least favorite escort. The glee on his face is downright panic inducing.

"Get your hands off me," I warn, my voice steady despite the adrenaline flooding my system.

He reaches for my clutch, but I twist in his grip, pulling it away just as another vibration pulses against my palm. The device is still working. Still pulling.

The guard's grip tightens, pain biting into my arm as he yanks me closer.

"No." I try to resist, even though my stupid pointy shoes make it next to impossible.

My heel catches, I stumble, and fuck... This is it, isn't it? This is how my life ends. Taken down by a pair of knockoff Louboutins.

What will my poor father think when he hears I was killed by a wannabe gangster in an underground sex club?

But before I make a face-plant, someone slides in behind me —quiet, firm, and sure. Two large hands close around my waist, anchoring me. Holding me up.

"Hands off," the man at my back says, his voice low and edged with something lethal.

Naturally, my body chooses this moment to short-circuit.

Heat flashes through me like it's been waiting for the excuse, my breath catches, and for one wildly reckless second, I have the insane urge to lean into him. To surrender to whatever dark power just wrapped itself around my waist like it owns me.

Because why not trade one threat for another?

The guard hesitates, his hold loosening, smug expression slipping, and gaze focused on the intruder.

I don't need to look behind me to know who it is. Still, I crane my neck to peek over my shoulder. And there he is.

The devil himself.

Exactly as I suspected.

He towers over me, his green eyes sharp and unyielding under the carved horns of his mask. His hands shift—one sliding low across my stomach, the other gripping my waist tighter. The touch is searing. Possessive.

It should rattle me. Instead, it anchors me. Emboldens me. Even as electricity skates across my skin.

But his gaze doesn't stray from the guard.

He leans forward, his chest pressing to my back, fingers flexing over my hip, and menace clear in every breath. "Now."

Chapter 7

Keir

Róisín trembles in my grip. She's soft and warm, and I can feel her heart hammering like she knows how close this is to turning bloody.

But she doesn't pull away. Doesn't try to fight.

No. The little rose leans in, spine straight, masked face tilted up to mine like a challenge. Fear buried beneath fire and steel.

Christ, she's stunning.

Up close, she's smaller than I thought. But her curves? They fit against me just right. Too fucking right. Like she was made to fill the space against me.

My cock's hard. My jaw's tight. My body's not thinking about the plan, the risk, or the potential bloodshed I've just triggered.

All it knows is her.

"She's mine." The words rip out of me, pure instinct laced with possession.

Her breath catches. Belly tightens under my palm. But she remains exactly where I want her.

It might just be survival. Might be calculation. Regardless, it feels like trust.

And I've no problem taking full advantage.

The arse-licker still clutching her squirms, looking to his boss for orders. Or backup.

But Bowen? That bastard just watches, cool as you like, a smirk tugging at his mouth. His lapdogs hover at his back, doing fuck all but watching, like this is part of the show.

Fucking cowards, the whole lot of them.

I lean toward the prick still holding her. "Last chance," I growl.

My hands tense. Rage coils in my spine.

I want to smash his jaw sideways. Shatter his nose. Drive a fist into his ribs and let the sound of it echo through every velvet-draped inch of this godforsaken club.

I want to make him bleed.

But I can't.

At least, not here. Not now.

One wrong move and I don't just blow my cover, I spark a war we don't walk away from. Gael might be family, but if I fuck with his business, he'll bury me.

And he'll toss the little rose in after.

"Let her go." Bowen flicks a wrist like she's a minor inconvenience. "No reason to make a scene."

The guard hesitates, then releases her with one last punishing squeeze. The angry red welt his fingers leave behind makes my blood fucking boil.

"Apologies for the interruption." I shove the fury down where it belongs. Keep my voice flat, my accent buried deep beneath years of practice. "She turns heads. Can't blame your man for getting distracted."

"Next time, keep a better leash on her." Bowen's voice drips with disdain.

There won't be a next time. If there is, I'll rip out his fucking throat. But I nod like a good little soldier and keep the peace. For now.

"Come on," I murmur at her ear, turning my back on the

bastard and his men, my hand settling firm at her waist. Right where it belongs.

My pulse pounds and free hand clenches to a tight fist, warding off the fury. It takes everything I've got not to turn around and crack skulls. Not to give in to the savage fucking itch clawing beneath my skin.

It's the kind of rage that doesn't listen to reason. The kind that gets men killed.

But I'm in control. Not the bloodlust. Not tonight.

I've got something more important in my grip.

And I'm not letting her go.

"You all right?" I ask, steering her through the shadows toward the back of the lounge.

She nods without looking at me, clutching her little bag to her chest like it's the only thing keeping her breathing.

And fuck, maybe it is. I'd bet good money whatever tech she's running is tucked inside, and she knows damn well she can't lose it. My uncle would have her fucking head.

Smart girl.

Too smart for this game. And far too tempting to walk away from.

I pick a booth far out of view of Bowen and his lackeys, with a clean sight line of the floor and a clear path to the exit. "Take a seat."

She hesitates, glancing toward her friends. They're still laughing, drinking, and have no idea how close she just came to becoming a casualty.

"Relax. It's just a drink. No strings. No expectations." I drop my voice lower. "Unless you're looking for some."

Color rises at the base of her throat, blooming like fire across her lovely chest. She holds my stare another second, then sighs and sinks into the velvet booth.

I don't waste time. I move in beside her, giving enough space she can leave if she likes, but close enough to keep her attention. To convince her to stay.

Shouldn't be hard. From the way she's responding—heat in her eyes, body leaning in—I'd say she's already made up her mind.

A server stops at our table, blonde hair pulled back and lace hugging her like a second skin. She's easy on the eyes and likely meant to distract from the money bleeding into this place.

But I don't even spare her a glance.

"Two whiskeys. Neat."

Róisín flashes me a glare—eyes narrowing and lips drawing tight.

"Something wrong?" I ask as the server glides toward the bar.

"Maybe I don't want whiskey. Maybe I don't even like it."

A laugh rumbles through my chest. Christ, she's sweet when she's bristling. "Drink it or don't. Hell, you've got a voice—order something else when she comes back."

She shifts beside me, legs pressed tight together, chin tipped high like she still has something to prove. Or maybe she's just holding herself together. Trying not to let me, or anyone, see the cracks in her armor. Trying to stay sharp. Untouchable.

Can't blame her. Not with that bastard's grip still burning on her skin, red and raw like a brand.

It gnaws at me. Scrapes something jagged and possessive loose inside my chest. Makes me want to lay my own marks across her skin. Ones she won't forget. And won't fucking want to.

The drinks arrive and I slide one toward her. Despite her earlier objection, she takes it without hesitation, downing half in one go.

I laugh again, low and rough, as the fight starts to seep out of my limbs.

"You claimed me. Like property." Her tone's brave, unforgiving, and has my cock fucking twitching in my pants. "What the hell was that about?"

A slow grin pulls at my mouth, and I tip my drink to hide it, watching her over the rim of the glass. Watching the frustration simmer—heating her cheeks, hardening her gaze, and building with each passing second of my silence.

Fucking gorgeous, this one. Goddamn glorious when she's pissed.

Finally, I set the glass down and lean in close enough to feel the heat bleeding off her skin. "I liked the way it sounded," I murmur, my gaze locked on hers.

She stares as though waiting for a deeper explanation, chest rising quick, breath snagging in her throat.

"And based on your reaction..." I dip my head, lips grazing her ear. "I'd say you liked it too."

Her mouth parts on a strangled cry. It's part protest, part confession.

And it's the prettiest fucking sound I've ever heard.

Chapter 8

Keir

The adrenaline's stopped pumping, but its effects still linger—tightening my chest, making my fingers twitch. I still want to wrap them around someone's throat.

Only now, it's not that bastard Bowen Alexander or his hired men I'm thinking about.

It's Róisín. Her pretty, delicate neck.

I want to feel her pulse jump under my palm. To see the fire in her eyes when I squeeze.

Not to silence her. Christ, no.

I want to hear her fucking scream.

"You liked the way it sounded? What's that supposed to mean?" She's got bite, but there's something softer beneath it. A flicker of doubt. Vulnerability wrapped in defiance.

Something I want to sink my teeth into.

"It means I didn't like the way that prick laid his hands on you." My voice is rough, but I hold my temper in check.

Because if I don't, I'll burn this whole place to the ground.

And I'd rather pour that heat into her.

Her eyes widen. "Why would you care? You don't even know me."

"No. But I'd like to." *Carnally.* "And call me old-fashioned, but I'm not the type to stand idly by while a woman gets assaulted. Not when I can do something to stop it."

She doesn't react, just keeps watching me with those sharp, calculating eyes. Like she's still weighing the odds. Still deciding whether I'm danger or deliverance.

A risk or a fucking reward.

Ah, my sweet little rose, I'm all of the above.

"So, is that your kink?" Her words are bold as brass, said with a secretive curve to her lips that makes my balls fucking ache.

I lift a brow. Not that she can see it behind this feckless mask. Hers hides too much as well. Christ, I'd tear them both off if I could.

I want her bare.

Not just stripped—laid open.

The job's likely done. I doubt she'd have followed me otherwise. But the game's far from over. Which means, the masks need to stay in place. My accent, hidden. And I'll just keep pretending this is all coincidence.

That I'm nothing more than a lucky bastard with great timing and a hard-on.

There's no other way to get what I want.

And what I want is Róisín. Any way I can fucking have her.

On her knees, her back, or bent over this table—I'm not picky. Whatever ends with my cock buried so deep she'll have trouble walking after.

"I could have dozens of kinks if you're involved. Which one did you have in mind?"

"None. That's not..." Her head shakes and that soft flush rises again, spreading slow across her chest like a fucking invitation. "I meant, it sounds like you enjoyed playing white knight."

"If that's what gets you off, I'll strap on some armor."

Her mouth snaps shut, jaw hardens, and fingers tense around her little purse. Either I've pushed too far or she's thinking about all the ways I could be making her come right now.

I run a finger over the rim of my glass, slow and taunting. Her gaze tracks the movement. Mouth parts. And Christ, I hope her mind's wandering the same delicious places as mine.

"You got a name?" I shift, adjusting myself and getting closer to her in one move.

She takes a slow sip of her drink, her eyes sliding away like she's deciding whether to give the truth or a lie.

Go on, little rose. Lie to me.

Her glass is nearly empty by the time she sets it down. But her hand's steady. Posture, taut. And she turns to meet my gaze head-on. "It's Robin."

Bold, clever fucking girl.

I'm glad she's protecting herself, not blindly handing over her identity or her trust.

But Robin?

Reminds me of the fairy tale. The prince of thieves, wasn't it? Stealing from the rich to feed the poor. Only tonight, she's feeding a different kind of beast. Taking from one monster to pay another.

My mouth twitches at the irony. "Robin?"

"Something funny?"

"No." I knock back my whiskey, taking pleasure as the burn slides down my throat. "Just trying it on. Feels a bit like a stage name."

She swallows hard, her breath stuttering.

"Don't worry," I murmur at her ear. "I don't care if it's real. I only wanted something to call you. And it's only for tonight."

"Tonight?"

"Yeah. One night. How's that sound?"

My gaze drags across her, lingering at the fluttering pulse in her throat. Noticing the slick pull of red satin over her breasts and hips. Savoring the way her body's torn between bolting and begging.

Her restraint's so thick I can fucking taste it.

And it makes me want to be the one to tear it away.

"Do I get a name for you?" she asks, voice growing soft. "For this one night?"

My grin spreads wide and wicked. "You can call me Devil."

"Of course I can." She rolls her eyes, giving me a sharp, bratty look that's too fucking perfect. "Is it meant to scare me? Are you trying to be dark and mysterious?"

"I don't have to try."

Her laugh is a bit breathless and pure goddamn sin.

I want to hear it again. Want to drag it out of her while she's gasping my name and writhing beneath me with her nails in my back. Make her eyes roll in her head for all the right reasons.

"What are you really doing here?" I ask like I don't already know. "This doesn't seem like your kind of place."

Yeah, it's a shite thing to press her like this, especially when I already know she didn't end up here by choice. But I need to be sure. Not about the mission—about her. About whether the danger turns her on.

Does she want out, or does some part of her want more? Want me?

"Let me guess..." Her mouth tips into a pretty, teasing smile. "This is your regular Friday night?"

Christ, if only. My nights, Fridays or otherwise, usually involve failing to keep one or more of my brothers sober after we've done something unsavory for my uncle. This? This is fucking luxury.

And her—sitting calm as you please after facing down real danger, all while strangers fuck in front of us?

She's a fucking gift.

"First time here," I tell her truthfully. "Not sure I plan on coming back. You?"

"After tonight?" She gives a dry little laugh. "Only if I'm dragged in blindfolded and drugged."

"Not your scene, then? The masks, leather, and ropes don't do it for you?"

Her gaze flicks to the show, then back to me, mouth curved

just slightly. "Oh, I don't know. The setup has potential. But what about you? Figured most men would pay good money for more of this place."

"I might." I press closer. "If their clientele weren't assholes, and the staff hadn't allowed you to get dragged upstairs like a party favor."

Her jaw clenches. "I had it handled."

She says it like she's daring me to argue, and fuck, maybe I should. But it's not fear in her eyes. It's fire. Controlled. Smoldering. The kind of flame that begs to be stoked.

She didn't come here for this. But she's not running either.

She's leaning in.

And that's all I need to know.

I shift even closer, my arm resting behind her, boxing her in without touching her. Letting her feel the cage without the lock. The power. And the fucking promise.

"And what about now, Robin?" My voice curls around the name like a hand around her throat. "Do you think you have me handled too?"

Her gaze drops to my mouth. "Oh, absolutely."

I move a hand to her bare knee, toying, testing, daring her to stop me.

But her breath catches even as her body relaxes under my touch.

She's not stopping a fucking thing.

"You knew exactly what you were doing when you put this dress on, didn't you?" I brush my lips over the shell of her ear.

"You like it?"

"I do. I bet it'd look great on the floor."

She hums in agreement, legs shifting and thighs parting.

"Now, tell me..." My body strains as I ignore temptation and continue tracing lazy patterns over her knee. "Are you mine for the night?"

A throaty little moan escapes her red lips.

But it's not enough. "Say it," I urge, my accent nearly slipping free.

Her head tilts toward me, breath warm against my mouth. Close enough to taste. Close enough to own.

"Say it," I whisper again, my fingers sliding along the slitted hem of her dress.

"All yours, Devil." Her voice is pure fucking fire. "But only for tonight."

I crush my mouth to hers, claiming the words, the heat, and the girl.

Swallowing her whole.

Game on, little rose.

Chapter 9

Róisín

The devil's mouth crashes into mine. And holy fucking hell, can the man kiss.

There's nothing hesitant about it. Nothing sweet. It's raw, unapologetic possession. He claims my lips like it's part of a plan. The next move in a game he's been playing since I walked into this club.

Honestly? It probably is.

The dramatic rescue, the righteous fury, the whole dark-and-mysterious act is all textbook manipulation. All to get me right here, right now, melting under his touch.

Well played, Devil, sir. Mission fucking accomplished.

Not that I'm naïve enough to mistake him for a hero. Not even close.

He's an opportunist. A wildcard. The kind of man who feeds on hope, desire, and need. He plays whatever role gets him closest to the prize, then disappears, leaving you wrecked and wondering if any of it was real.

That won't be me. Not this time.

My eyes are wide open.

His hand grips my thigh, fingers digging into my skin with the kind of authority that doesn't ask permission. The other tangles at the back of my neck, holding me in place while he takes and takes and fucking takes.

But I'm not just along for the ride. I give it right back.

I arch into him, hand curling over his shoulder as I pull him closer, inviting danger with every stroke of my tongue.

He tastes like whiskey and sin, setting me on fire from the inside. Burning through me until I'm too hot to think, and too far gone to care.

Because when he kisses, it's chaos.

Code-breaking, system-crashing, full-tilt overload.

And who the hell turns that down?

I should care that we're in public. That the booth's not really private and everyone could be watching. That I barely escaped Bowen's clutches with all my limbs intact.

But all I can think about is the scrape of his stubble, the dominance of his touch, and the weight of his body pressing me into the velvet seat like a delicious promise.

His hand slides higher, fingers trailing the inside of my thigh with excruciating patience. Like he's savoring every second of the inevitable victory.

Because yeah, I'm soaked. And I have no doubt he knows it.

The throb between my thighs deepens, sharpened by the symphony of sex playing out behind every curtain. Moans. Gasps. Leather creaking. Flesh meeting flesh with a slap that echoes in the dark.

And God, I want more. Need more.

It doesn't matter that I don't know this man's name or even what he looks like. Or that all I'll remember is a mask, a voice, and the rough touch of his hands. It's enough.

Because for this one impulsive night, we want the same thing.

To feel.

To step outside the bounds of predictable, everyday life, and experience this moment for what it is. A break in the pattern. A filthy fantasy come to life.

And most likely, a beautiful fucking mistake.

His mouth drags down the column of my throat, teeth scoring hard enough to make me gasp. He lingers there, breathing me in like he's trying to memorize the way I taste and the way I sound when I'm unraveling beneath him.

"If it's too much, tell me to stop," he says against my throat, sending another shiver straight to my core.

I should. I should shove him back, slap some sense into myself, remember exactly why I came here tonight. Why I shouldn't still be hanging around.

But God help me, I can't.

Not when every nerve ending in my body is lit up like a goddamn circuit board.

Instead, I tilt my chin, give him better access, and whisper, "Don't you dare."

A rumble vibrates in his chest, pleased and dangerous. The kind of sound that says I better hold on tight because he's about to ruin me.

His hand finally slips beneath the hem of my dress, dragging the fabric up, baring more and more until the cool air kisses the tops of my thighs. And then his fingers do too. A single knuckle, brushing just shy of where I need it.

I bite back a whimper, clutching the lapel of his jacket like it holds the last shred of my self-control.

Spoiler... It doesn't.

"Is this what you want?" He grazes my silk-covered mound, fingers dragging along the edge of my panties as if he's got all the time in the world. "The devil's hand on your pretty cunt?"

A moan escapes before I can stop it.

He chuckles. *Bastard.*

I should feel exposed. Maybe even embarrassed. But all I feel is power, coiled deep and electric. Because if he thinks I'm just going to lie back, he's in for a surprise.

I drag his mouth back to mine, tasting my own desperation on his tongue. The side of my mask digs into my cheek, and I welcome the sting. Fuck, I'd let it bleed if it meant he'd stop teasing and put those hands to proper use.

"Touch me," I demand against his lips, done pretending. "Or I swear to God, I'll do it myself."

I can feel his grin against my mouth, full of dark amusement and filthy intent. "Greedy little thing, aren't you?"

"Do you have a problem with that?"

"Hell no." He laughs again, low and rough, the sound stroking down my spine. "Just wondering if you're always like this."

I pull back, my stomach tightening with the tiniest flicker of unease. Am I too intense? Too demanding? He wouldn't be the first man to decide I was.

Although, that other man was a useless asshole.

"Like what?" I ask, even though I'm not sure I want the answer.

"Unapologetic."

Well. That's a new one.

"You mean shameless?" The words come out a little breathless, my body still wound tight.

"I mean fucking irresistible." He leans in, masked nose brushing mine. "You walked in here like you were prepared to set the place on fire, are demanding what you want like it's already yours"—his lips land a soft kiss over mine—"and made me hard the moment I saw you."

My answering smile feels wicked and seductive. "Really? You were hard for me?"

"Still am, shameless girl," he says like it's praise. "I just hope you can handle what you're asking for."

"Not only can I handle it, but I think I've earned a little indulgence. Don't you?"

He doesn't respond to that. Doesn't move either. Just watches me like I'm some kind of riddle he's in no rush to solve. Which would be fine, if I wasn't practically begging him to undo me.

All I want are his hands, his mouth, and that hard cock he's teasing me with. Whatever he'll give me. I need it.

Because if the job didn't work—if I didn't get everything Gael O'Shea wants—I could be a dead woman walking. There won't be a second chance for this. Or anything else.

So, am I going to be greedy? Shameless? Indulgent?

Damn right I am.

If all that's guaranteed is this one moment, this one night, then I'm not just going to take it...I'm going to fucking own it. I'll become the confident, take-no-shit woman I've been playing.

I slide my hand over his, pressing it right between my thighs. "So, are you going to touch me now, or what?"

Chapter 10

Keir

Shameless as fucking hell.

I picked up on her bravery the second she walked in—calculating and ready for danger, like she knew the rules and planned to break them all. But this?

This is a whole new game.

The way she watches me, anticipating my next move. The heat of her hand over mine, dragging it right where she wants it, bold as you like. As if she's the one calling the shots, and I'm the one getting played.

Fuck, maybe I am.

Maybe she's not the innocent girl, paying off her brother's debt like I was told. It's unlikely, but she could be a spy for my uncle. A test of my obedience. The perfect goddamn lure, dressed to ruin and sent to see if I'll bite.

And maybe I don't give a shite.

Because even if every word out of her mouth is a lie, the need dripping from her like a promise isn't. The sodden silk sticking to her skin?

Yeah, not a chance in hell she's faking that.

Or the moan that catches in her throat when I curl my fingers around the side of her panties and pull.

I drag the fabric up, shifting it side to side. Toying with her. Letting it dig into her skin just enough to leave a mark.

Christ, I'm wound tight—jaw clenched, cock throbbing, and blood pounding in my ears. I want to drop to my knees and devour her. Face first. Tongue deep. Make her scream so loud the whole room turns to listen.

But I'm not rushing this.

Not when I know how it ends.

Because she's the job, and I've already crossed a line. There's no after. No second round. Anything more than this would gut the life I've built and leave me bleeding in the wreckage.

So, if one night, one stolen taste is all I get, I'm going to make it count. Make it fucking last. Drag her over every edge. Burn every gasp and moan into my brain until they're carved there.

I lower my mouth to her neck. "And how exactly would you like me to touch you?" Land a kiss to her throat. "Slow?" And another. "Fast and rough?"

Then one more as I tug her panties hard. "Spread wide over the table for the whole room to see?"

I let the fabric snap back into place and pull my hand away, watching her face for the fallout. Her breath hitches and gaze flickers, full of heat, tension, and something primal.

But then her eyes dart to the crowd. The thrum at her throat pulses harder, wild and frantic, like her body just caught up to the fact that we're not alone. That every eye in this godforsaken club could be on us.

Is she going to lose her nerve? Reconsider?

If she does, it's only for a second. Because when she looks at me again, there's nothing soft in her stare. It's all fire and hunger. A spark that dares me to feed it.

"Do you think they're watching?" she whispers, voice like fucking sin.

There's no fear in it. Just thrill.

Seems my sweet little rose likes the idea of an audience.

"Maybe. Does that turn you on?" I drag my hand up her

thigh again, only stopping when I hit silk. "Do you want to give them a show?"

"I want you to make me forget they exist." She shifts her legs open, rolling her hips into my hand like she owns the moment. "What do you say, Devil? Are you up to the task?"

A slow grin curls across my lips as I grab the crook of her knee and drag it up into my lap, spreading her wide for me.

We're tucked into the shadows, the table shielding most of what matters. Anyone looking would have to be real fucking bold to catch more than a glimpse.

But the idea of it—the risk, the claim, and the chance to show every bastard in this room that tonight, she chose me? Fuck, that lights something in me.

I've never been one for the spotlight. In my world, too much attention gets you clipped. But with her thighs spread and my hand between them, I want the whole room to feel it.

To know she's mine.

And Christ, I want to take her—hard, raw, and reckless. I want to push her back, rip that silk to shreds, and fuck her until she doesn't just forget the gawkers, but her own name. How to breathe. Everything but me.

Instead, I slip a finger beneath the wet strip of silk and drag it aside, exposing her pretty cunt, glistening in the low light. Slick and ready.

Goddamn perfect.

I slide two fingers through her heat, slow and punishing, before circling her clit. She twitches at the contact, hips jerking and breath catching. But she doesn't look away.

She holds my gaze. Eyes blazing. Lips parted. Begging me without a word to take it further.

So I give her what she's asking for.

I drive my fingers into her without warning or mercy. Deep, brutal, and unforgiving.

And Christ, even drenched as she is, she's still tight.

She whimpers, clamping down around my digits like she's

already on the edge. Pulsing. Desperate. Like her cunt knows exactly what it wants and isn't shy about taking it.

My cock throbs, hard as fucking stone, straining against my zipper. Just the thought of burying myself in her, stretching her wide, has my jaw clenched and every inch of me aching.

It's going to be savage. A raw, glorious fucking squeeze.

"Is this what you wanted?" I murmur, voice low and thick in her ear. "My fingers buried in your cunt while half the room pretends not to notice?"

She whimpers again.

Fucking hell. That sound—wrecked and raw—goes straight to my spine.

She tightens around me, her body answering without hesitation, and it's all I can do not to take her right here and now.

But not yet.

Not until she's surrendered, coming on my hand with her legs shaking, teeth biting down on that filthy little moan she's desperate to let loose.

Not until I've wrung every drop of pleasure from her just like this. Open. Bold. Loving every second of it.

And all fucking mine.

Chapter 11

Róisín

There's no coming back from this.

Not when his fingers are buried so deep, I can feel the rough drag of his palm at my entrance. Not when I'm balanced on the edge of orgasm in a room full of strangers, legs spread, mask slipping, and heart pounding so hard it feels like it's about to shatter something inside me.

And the devil hasn't even moved yet.

"Look at you," he growls against my neck. "Squirming in my hand. Desperate for it."

His fingers shift, just enough to make me gasp, before he pulls back with a slow, punishing stroke. Every inch drags against my walls, wet and aching, like he's trying to make me feel the loss.

"You want to come so badly, don't you?"

I nod, dizzy with need.

But that's not good enough for him.

"Say it."

"Yes," I breathe. "Fuck, I need to—"

He slams back into me, and I suck in a breath so sharp it stings.

"You need to what?" His thumb presses against my clit, circling like he already knows exactly how to set me off. "Need to come? Need to soak my fingers while the whole fucking club watches?"

I whimper, my legs trembling and brain short-circuiting.

Honestly? I don't even care if anyone's watching. Let them enjoy every depraved second. I don't give a damn anymore.

In fact, I hope they're jealous.

Because I want it too much. Want him too much.

And I don't even know his name.

My hips roll on instinct, chasing pressure like a bitch in heat—wild, needy, and way past pretending otherwise. One hand fists the lapel of his jacket, while the other grips the back of the booth, holding on for balance. Or for dear fucking life.

"More," I beg, my voice as broken as I feel.

Thank fuck and bad decisions, he listens.

His fingers curl deep inside me, hitting that perfect spot with ruthless precision, making me tremble so violently I'm seconds from losing it.

It's not just pleasure, it's reprogramming. A brutal rewrite of everything I thought I could control.

"You're a fucking mess already, and I've barely started." He bites at the underside of my jaw, eliciting another shock of pleasure. "You'll let me do whatever I want, won't you?"

"Yes." It rips out of me, raw and helpless feeling.

Because Lord fucking help me, it's true.

"You'll take everything I give you. Let me bend you over this booth. Fuck you so hard the table shakes. Let them all hear what a filthy little whore you are for me."

"Yes." The word scrapes out of me, caught between a gasp and a prayer. "Only for you."

He groans, low and savage. "Only for me."

But it's not a vow. It's a fucking command.

And I feel it everywhere. In the clutch of my pussy, the sting in my throat, the wild, frantic need clawing at my insides.

Like he means to ruin me, and I'm ready to let him.

His fingers drive deeper, rougher, building fast—almost too

fast—until I'm right there, trembling, gasping, begging for the fall.

And just when I'm about to tip, he pulls back.

Slows down.

Leaves me dangling on the edge, shaking and starved, one heartbeat away from ripping the control from his hands and riding his fingers just to finish myself off.

"You think I'm going to let you come that easy?" he rasps, voice thick with want as he drags his fingers out of me again. "Not when you sound like that."

I moan—loud and unguarded—and he fucking shudders, like he's feeding off it. Like every needy sound I make goes straight to his cock.

"Christ, I like it when you beg." He flicks his tongue over my ear, his breath hot against my skin. "Could listen to it all night. The way you crave me. You're going to sound so pretty when you come."

My hips jerk, desperate for him to give it back. For him to fill me again. "Then do it," I hiss. "Touch me. Make me come."

But instead of obeying, he grins. "Nah. Not yet."

He presses his palm against my inner thigh, keeping me spread and writhing, while his other hand snakes up my torso, grabbing a handful of my silk-covered breast. His touch is possessive, patient, and downright cruel.

"You want it? Then tell me how good I make you feel. Tell me no one's ever touched you like this. No one's ever ravaged you like I can."

My throat tightens. My pride flares. But my body? My body's a traitor—shaking, soaked, and begging him with every twitch.

"Say it," he growls. "Say I'm the only man that's ever had you spread and dripping this way."

I turn my head, lips brushing his, and whisper, "You are."

"Louder."

"You're the best," I gasp, flushed and ruined. "Fuck, no one's ever—"

His fingers slam back into me, and I scream. Only, the sound gets swallowed as his mouth crashes against mine.

It's not sweet. It's not soft.

It's savage.

A ravenous claim that devours my cry and turns it into something even dirtier. His tongue tangles with mine, stealing the breath from my lungs as his hand fucks me mercilessly, forcing wave after wave of pleasure until I'm nothing but sensation.

Helpless. Drenched.

And completely his.

Chapter 12

Róisín

I sink back against the booth, legs still spread, dress hitched high, heart hammering like it's trying to reboot.

The rest of the world is gone. There's no music, moans, or dark velvet chaos. Just a muted quiet, like I've been dropped into some post-orgasm blackout zone.

I can't think. Can't breathe. Can't believe I just let that happen. In public.

Fuck, who am I kidding?

I didn't just let it happen—I spread my legs and pleaded for it.

A stranger finger-fucked me senseless while calling me his filthy little whore, and I fucking loved it. Thanked him for it. Played along and asked for more.

Maybe guilt will catch up later. But right now? Whatever moral compass I had is corrupted and unrecoverable.

I feel high. Almost giddy. Free in a way I don't have the code to process.

Sure, I'm raw, flushed, and a bit unsteady. But this is the most alive I've felt in...

Ever.

Not that the bar was high. My usual Friday night thrill

involves bypassing email protections and defending the *Twilight* saga in chat rooms. The books, obviously—I'm not a monster.

In my defense, I never once in my twenty-five years imagined myself in a place like this. Enjoying an exhibitionist kink. With a man I just met.

A man who's still watching me like I'm exactly where I belong.

His deep green gaze doesn't waver. It's dark. Greedy. He's unapologetically sure of himself. And he has every fucking right to be.

Although, judging by the rock-hard press of his cock against my leg, I'm guessing he's not nearly as satisfied as he looks.

Good. Let him suffer a little. He deserves it after the way he teased me.

He drags his fingers in a slow line over my inner thigh, leaving a slick path that makes me shiver. Then lifts them to his mouth and licks them clean, his eyes locked on mine.

And smiles. "Just how I like it."

I swallow hard, scrambling for something clever to say. Something to tip the scales back in my direction.

"I don't usually do this," I admit. Not exactly the knockout line I was aiming for.

His smirk is slow and wicked. Far too fucking pleased. "No one ever does."

The words settle like a spark in my chest—daring and electric. And suddenly, I don't feel uncertain. I feel unstoppable.

Still unsteady, thighs slick from what he just did to me, I slide closer. My dress stays bunched around my hips, showing off the mess he's made. But I'm not bothering to fix it.

He says nothing. Just watches, jaw tight, gaze dragging over me like he's trying to memorize every inch.

"If you're going to stare," I murmur, "I might as well give you something worth remembering."

His eyes flick up, sharp and hungry.

"You're done teasing now." I trail a finger over his stubbled jaw. "My turn."

His eyes narrow. "Is that right?"

I slide my hand down his chest, over the firm plane of his stomach, straight to where he's hard and waiting. No hesitation. No subtlety. I've got plans, and this place isn't open all night.

"That's exactly right." I swing a leg over his lap and straddle him.

He shifts beneath me, making room like he's been waiting for this since the moment I walked in.

I squeeze my hand around the outline of his cock as I stretch my thighs wide over his.

He hisses through his teeth. "Careful, shameless girl."

"I don't want careful." I lean in, brushing my lips over his.

And then I kiss him. Hard.

His hands snap to my hips, his fingers digging into my flesh—brutal and possessive. He groans into my mouth, and I swallow the sound, my silk-covered pussy joining my hand to rock against the thick, solid pressure of his cock through his pants.

He's so hard it hurts to move. But I do it anyway, grinding down again and again until his breath turns ragged and his grip bruises.

"Fuck," he growls, breaking the kiss. "You want it that bad?"

"Yes," I pant. "Right here. Right now."

He grins like a wolf. "Then ride me. Take what you want. Show me how desperate you are for my cock."

I don't wait.

My fingers go to his belt, fumbling once before I get it undone. He lifts his hips, helping me drag the zipper down.

Then he's there, straining against his boxers, thick and hot and impossible to ignore.

My pulse stutters as I tug them down and close my fingers around him. He's heavy in my palm, flushed dark, already slick at the tip.

And he's big. Maybe too big. And so hard, I know it's going to hurt.

God, it's going to hurt so fucking good.

He groans as my other hand joins the first, stroking him slowly.

"Fuck, you're eager," he mutters, head tipping back against the booth.

"Still think I'm too polite for this place?" I ask, guiding him exactly where I need him, pushing my panties aside to slick his length through my wetness.

He lets out a ragged laugh. "Not even a little."

"You've got protection?" I ask, breathless but clear.

He blinks like he's catching up, then nods. "Jacket pocket. Left side."

I reach for it, digging into sleek black fabric until my fingers close around foil, then tearing it open fast. I might be aching for him, but I'm not giving my body away completely. Not even for one reckless night.

He groans when I roll it down over him—purposely slow, just to hear that sound again.

"Now you're going to be a tease?" he mutters.

"You started it."

I line him up, shift my hips, and sink down onto him in one long, torturous slide.

The stretch steals my breath. He fills me too fast, too full, too fucking deep, hitting that edge of pain that borders on addictive.

My body clamps down, tight and pulsing, and he swears beneath me. "Jesus—fuck—"

I don't give either of us time to recover. I start to move, taking everything I want.

My pace. My rules.

And he lets me.

Until someone screams.

It's loud, raw, and filled with ecstasy. A sound that echoes through the room and snaps me out of the moment.

Everything comes rushing back. The noise. The bodies. The velvet booth and the slick press of skin on skin. It all hits me at once.

Too sharp. Too real.

I can't see them, but I can feel them. The crowd. The heat. The pulse of bass and breath and sex behind me.

We're just another act in the dark.

That shouldn't bother me. Hell, it hasn't stopped me so far.

But something catches in my chest—tight and breathless—and for a second, I falter. My hips stop rolling, pulse spikes for the wrong reason, and gaze darts to the mirror on the wall above us, trying in vain to see who's watching.

"Eyes on me." His voice cuts through the distraction, low and rough, like a secret meant just for me.

I look at him.

Masked. Steady. Gorgeous in the dark.

"You feel this?" he murmurs, fingers sliding between my legs, finding the spot where we're joined. "This is all that matters. This is you and me. The rest of it's just decoration."

"But—" I start, breath catching hard.

"We're both masked," he says, calm and certain, recognizing my panic before I do. "They don't know who we are. And they don't fucking matter."

His thumb finds my clit and circles slow. Like sin and salvation all at once.

I bite back a moan. My legs are shaking, my body stretched full around him, and my mind scrabbles for something solid as the ground shifts again.

"If they're watching, you're the only thing they'll remember." His free hand slides up my back, grounding me. "So, come on, shameless girl, give them a fucking show."

The words detonate inside me.

My hips move on instinct—raw, greedy, chasing the sound he makes when I take him deep.

And still, he lets me lead.

He watches me like he's enchanted by my every move. Every breath. Every fuck-drunk smile and sound.

Even now, part of me still can't believe I'm doing this. Still can't believe I want this.

But God, I do.

I want to come again, right here, riding him in this velvet-draped room full of sex and strangers, like I don't have anything to lose.

Because even if I do—even if the plan worked and my life resets to normal in the morning—isn't the best sex of my life worth it?

Chapter 13

Keir

She moves like we're alone. Just the two of us in our own private world.

No panic. No doubt. Just the slow, filthy drive of a woman who knows exactly what she wants and isn't afraid to take it.

Sure, she's still trembling from that slip when the over-the-top scream from the floor show nearly ruined everything. It rattled her. Shook her rhythm. Had her questioning herself.

She could've pulled away. Could've frozen, folded, or begged me to stop.

But she didn't.

One filthy whisper in her ear and she looked me straight in the eye, clamped those perfect thighs tighter around my waist, and continued to ride me like it's a holy calling. Like her need to get off outweighs all the risks. Fuck the consequences.

And Christ, that does something dark to my head.

Because what she said—about not normally doing this? It wasn't just a line.

This isn't some performance. She's not faking it for the voyeurs or even for me. Every roll of her hips, every moan she bites back, every shudder that rips through her is real.

And it's all for her.

Which, somehow, makes it mine too.

Because she's handing it over, raw and unguarded—the part of her I crave more than the slick heat between her legs. That dark, dangerous hunger that matches mine.

It pulses through everything she does. The way she braces her hands on my shoulders, fingers curling in my jacket like she needs something solid to hold on to. The flush high on her cheeks, barely concealed by the mask. And her lips, parted and soft, every time she sinks down and takes me deep.

I run a hand over her tits, wishing I could tear her dress open and feast on her properly. But I want her walking out of here the same way she came in—composed, head high, looking like no one ever touched her.

Even if I'm buried deep inside her while I think it.

Because yeah, I might be fucking her in front of a crowd, but the thought of someone else seeing her like this makes me want to stab something.

"Please. I need more." Christ, she's a fucking vision when she begs.

I feel it in every desperate roll of her hips. She's chasing that high like her life depends on it. But she's not going to get there on her own.

I give her breast one last squeeze before moving my hand up and wrapping it around her throat like a collar.

This isn't a threat. Or control.

It's a claim, plain and simple. A silent promise that tells her exactly who the fuck she belongs to.

Her breath catches. Eyes lock on mine. And fuck, the look she gives me is so wild, so fucking glorious, it has my balls drawing tighter with each passing second.

Because it's not fear I see in her pretty gaze.

It's surrender.

She clenches around me—hot and soaked and so fucking tight it makes me dizzy.

Still, I don't take over. Not yet.

I want her to keep going. I want her to come again like this, riding me at her own speed, wearing my hand like a necklace.

Her rhythm falters. Hips stutter. Breath catches. Thighs shake. She's right there, so fucking close. Only holding on by a thread.

I keep my hand at her throat, firm but careful, letting her feel it. Letting her know she's safe to fall apart in my hands.

She bows forward, her masked face brushing the side of mine, close enough that her breath spills across my cheek.

"Come on," I murmur, voice low and strained. "Take it."

A moan slips from her lips, and I tighten my grip just slightly, just enough to tip her over the edge.

And then she's gone.

She jerks hard, thighs locking around me as the orgasm slams through her—raw, violent, and fucking glorious. Her movements turn sloppy as she chases every wave with broken little moans that make my cock throb like hell. Then she drops down hard, her cunt spasming around me, soaked and squeezing tight.

That's it. That's the fucking trigger.

My control snaps.

I grip her waist and thrust up into her, deep and rough, burying myself to the hilt as I come. Hard. I spill into the condom while she pulses around me, still trembling, still gasping against my throat.

My vision blacks out for a second. My jaw locks. I growl something feral into her neck, not even sure what the fuck I just said.

She collapses against me, wrecked and breathless, and I wrap an arm around her back to keep her from sliding off my lap.

I let my head fall back against the booth, chest heaving, cock still buried inside her. Her body twitches through the aftershocks.

She shifts against me, curling in like she knows I'll protect her. Like the trust is fucking real.

Like this perfect thing between us can last.

"You should see yourself right now," I murmur, stroking a hand through her glossy auburn hair.

She stirs, lifts her gaze to mine, and offers the softest, sweetest smile. "Am I a mess?"

"A beautiful one," I tease. "You look like your world's just been rocked off its axis."

And fuck, even as I say it, something pangs deep in my chest. Because this is the only time I'll ever get to see her this way. The first and the last.

There's no choice in the matter.

I'm not a soft man—I'll get over the loss.

But right now, even with her still in my arms, it feels a bit like a death sentence.

Chapter 14

Róisín

My body's still running hot, but the high's bleeding out fast, and my brain's clawing its way back online. Except, it's laggy and glitching like it just survived a hard crash.

What the hell did I just do?

Scratch that. I know exactly what I did. That's the problem.

I shift in the devil's lap, suddenly hyperaware of everything—the cool air against my sweat-slicked skin, the damp stickiness between my thighs, the bass still pulsing through the walls like a heartbeat out of sync.

My mask itches, but at least it's holding up. Which is more than I can say for my dress, currently halfway to useless. I tug it down without ceremony. There's no need for grace. Only damage control.

He moves too, finally, reaching across the table to grab a handful of cocktail napkins from the silver tray. He doesn't hesitate, doesn't even try for gentleness. He's practical. His motions efficient. As though he's closing out the bar tab, instead of recuperating after smashing my world.

Without a word, he cleans up. Condom off, wrapped tight, a few swipes to erase the evidence, then tucking himself back into his pants like nothing happened.

"There's more." He holds out the extras, his tone flat. "I can help if you want."

The offer's not crude. Or sexy. Or even smug. Just matter-of-fact. Like he's offering tech support. Or pointing out the nearest exit.

My gaze sticks on the napkins as I take them, doing my best to pretend this is all very normal. "Thanks, I've got it covered."

Sure I do. Casual sex with a masked stranger? Totally routine.

Fuck. I feel like I've just landed in someone else's skin and am still figuring out the controls. But I fix my panties, smooth my dress, and slide off his lap like it's no big deal. Like I've done this a dozen times before.

At least my body remembers how to fake composure, even if my mind is still scrambled.

I slip into the booth beside him, a little too aware of every inch of skin, every brush of fabric, and every eye that might still be watching me fumble my way through the aftermath.

The noise of the room creeps back in. The music. The bodies. The hum of pleasure all around us, pulsing like background code I'd tuned out.

"I should probably..." My words stall as I reach for my clutch, fingers tightening around it as if it can anchor me in the real world.

Because what just happened between us? That was a fantasy. A deviant side quest. And I'm just now buffering back into reality.

Truth is, I have no idea what I'm supposed to say. Or do. There's no protocol. No fallback script. There's only a whole lot of awkward and a gnawing question I don't have the balls to ask.

Now that the deed is done and the promise kept, what the hell comes next?

One-night stands aren't exactly my thing, but I'm pretty sure they don't end with a cuddle and a conversation.

"No need to rush off." His voice cuts clean through the static

—calm, smooth, and totally untouched by the chaos he just pulled out of me.

My gaze lifts, meeting his for the first time since I came apart in his lap.

And yep, just as I feared, even with the mask and that infuriating composure, he's still hot enough to ruin me. Still tempting enough to make me say yes to things I should absolutely walk away from.

"Stay," he says, nodding toward the table. "Have another drink. We've got time."

He doesn't wait for my answer, just raises two fingers and, voilà, the server appears with another round like she's been summoned by magic or sexual dominance. Whiskey for him. Something light and sparkling for me, even though I never placed an order.

I take a sip, anyway, letting the burn ground me. Because what else am I going to do? Walk out dazed and disheveled like I just rage quit a porn set?

His eyes stay on me. Not devouring like before, but focused. Steady. As if he's making sure I'm still functional.

Maybe it should make me feel self-conscious. Instead, I'm just confused—my mind stuck and refusing to clear.

Two words loop on repeat.

Not just words, but an endearment. A nickname.

And not just any nickname. One that just happens to match the meaning of my real name. The one I know for a fact I never gave him.

Words he might not have meant to say out loud. But in the middle of all that heat and friction, right as he came, I'm almost certain I heard him whisper it.

Little rose.

I stare down into my drink, pulse ticking in my throat.

Could've been anything. A glitch in my memory. Delusion. Coincidence. Maybe it's his go-to closer, something he calls every woman he fucks—right after *baby* and *good girl*.

But it wasn't just what he said. It's the way he said it.

With a lovely Irish lilt.

That was definitely not my imagination. I'd know that accent anywhere, since I grew up with it ringing through the damn walls of my house. Hell, if it weren't for my American mother and a school system obsessed with assimilation, I'd probably have it myself.

I glance at him from the corner of my eye.

He looks relaxed. One arm slung over the back of the booth, posture casual, gaze unreadable. Like this is just another night, just another drink, and I'm just another girl he won't remember tomorrow.

But something's off. Those words won't dislodge. And the intent way he's watching me only makes it worse. Doubt simmers beneath the surface, whispering warnings I should've paid attention to hours ago.

Too bad hindsight doesn't come with an undo button.

"You good?" He shifts closer, his pinky tracing over the back of my hand. "You seem a little..."

"I'm fine." The lie slides out on instinct. I exhale slowly, masking the panic trying to claw its way up my spine. "No regrets."

His mouth ticks up. "Not even a little?"

I shake my head. "Not right now."

And that part, at least, is honest. Whatever hell waits on the other side of this night, I don't regret what happened. Not yet.

He nods, like he respects the answer. Like he expected me to fall apart instead.

I swirl the drink in my hand, watching the bubbles rise and break. The silence between us stretches, thick with something I can't name. Something that should probably scare me.

But after what we just did—the way he wrung that mind-bending orgasm out of me like it was nothing? Please. Fear's not even in the top ten things I'm feeling right now. Not when he already had his hand around my throat.

Hell, for all I know he's a hitman. Or married, with a mortgage and three kids. But as soon as I walk out of here, none of it matters. This doesn't follow us home.

Still, those words niggle in the back of my brain. *Little rose.*

"Is it out of place for me to ask where you're from? Does it break too many rules?"

He doesn't answer right away. Just tilts his head, studying me through the mask like he's running diagnostics.

"Why do you want to know?"

I give a casual shrug. "Curiosity, I guess. I've never done anything like this with a stranger before. Figured knowing something about you might help me feel a little less like a slut."

His jaw hardens. "You think knowing my hometown would change anything?"

"No," I say, too fast, too defensive.

"Then don't dress it up. Don't try to turn it into something neat and explainable. It doesn't make you a slut because you wanted to feel good." His voice is low but certain. No shame. No softness. Just fact delivered with that maddening calm.

And fine, maybe he has a point.

Still, something in the air between us feels off. Like a puzzle that almost clicks but not quite.

"Robin?" The voice cuts through my thoughts, loud enough to make me jump.

Kayla.

She stumbles into view at the edge of the booth—heels dangling from one hand, eyes wide, hot-pink hair messy, and breath ragged. Sweat clings to her skin, and panic is etched into every line of her face.

Everything tilts.

Her gaze flicks from me to the devil beside me, taking in the scene without comment. No questions. No judgment. Just sheer, unfiltered fear as she grips the edge of the table like it might keep her standing.

"I've been looking everywhere," she gasps. "Something's wrong."

I shift across the bench toward her. "What happened?"

"It's Liv." Her voice breaks as tears flood her eyes. "She's gone. I can't find her."

My hand closes over hers, hoping to calm her. But the contact only amplifies her dread and pours it straight into me.

"When did you last see her?"

"I don't know. Twenty minutes ago? Maybe longer." She shakes her head, scanning the shadows like Liv might pop out with a grin and a cocktail. "We were getting drinks. Then she said she had to pee. I waited, but she never came back. I thought maybe she got distracted, but now..."

But now it's been too long. And this place is littered with red flags—the exact kind that would call to a chaos addict like Liv.

I rise from the booth and squeeze her hand, already switching into problem-solving mode. "We'll find her."

Heat presses in behind me as the devil stands, jacket falling into place as though we've just wrapped up a boardroom negotiation, instead of fucking like animals in public. His solid hand settles at my waist, claiming me with a single touch.

And despite the adrenaline racing through my system and the fact that this isn't remotely the time, it still lights a fire low in my belly.

"I can help." His voice is quiet but resolute.

Kayla looks him over—broad chest, sharp suit, that wicked mask—and her eyes flick to me with a silent question. One she doesn't have to say out loud.

Unlike me, her reaction to him is sensible. Wary. Probably the response you're supposed to have to a masked stranger with boundary issues.

I don't know who he is. Don't know his name, his game, or what lies behind the mask.

But I know what he did. He pulled me away from Bowen and

his men before anything worse could happen. He might not be a white knight, but he fucking saved me.

And the way he's watching us now isn't predatory or malicious.

It's protective.

I nod. "Okay. You take the VIP level. Kayla and I will go back through the main lounge."

He inclines his head, mask catching the light. "I'll check the back rooms, too, and talk to the staff."

I almost laugh.

Seriously, why does he have to be decent? If he were just an asshole, walking away would be so much easier. Hell, I might even be able to forget him.

But no. He has to go and ruin it by being good.

"You with me?" I ask Kayla.

She nods, but her fingers are still trembling in mine.

The devil leans in, his breath warm against my ear. "If she's still here, I'll find her. I promise."

And despite everything—the sweat cooling on my skin and the doubt creeping into my bones—I believe him.

We break apart.

I grab Kayla's hand and weave us through the crowd, heart pounding against my ribs like it's trying to outrun the dread.

Liv might be chaos incarnate, but that doesn't mean she shouldn't have someone watching her back. Someone who gives a damn. I only met her tonight, but somehow, she already feels like mine to look after.

They both do.

That's where my focus should be. My friends.

But before we even reach the halfway point, I glance back over my shoulder. Just once.

Searching for him.

His broad shoulders. That deliberate stride. The mask I already know will haunt me.

I don't know what I'm hoping for—one last look, a lingering stare, maybe even a reckless kiss goodbye—but all I catch is his back as he disappears into the dark.

Chapter 15

Róisín

The curtain parts, and we step into the main lounge like we've crossed dimensions.

Gone is the hush of the back room—the velvet, the shadows, the soft moans swallowed by dark corners. Out here, it's all gold, glitter, and mayhem. Light flashes. Bass slams through the floor. Laughter cuts through the air, loud and jagged.

The party's in full swing.

Drinks are flowing. People are dancing. Flirting. Lounging half-draped over each other like we're hours into the kind of night no one will remember clearly. And if they do, they'll swear they don't.

It's bright. Overstimulating.

And completely at odds with the panic coiled tight in my gut.

Kayla's still got a death grip on my hand, nails biting deep. It hurts, but I welcome it. The sting keeps me present. And it's a little reminder of what can happen when you take unnecessary risks.

We sweep the room booth by booth, corner by corner. I scan every face, every outfit, hunting for blonde hair, a white dress, that charismatic grin that says *this is probably a mistake.*

And find nothing.

We push past the bathrooms. The photo wall. The damn champagne tower that just keeps on flowing. But there's still no sign of her, and it makes me think something is very, very wrong.

We circle the room twice more.

Still no Liv. No fucking trace she was ever here.

And somewhere in the back of my mind, beneath the noise and rising panic, I wonder if the devil's had any better luck.

He said he'd help. And I believed him.

Not because I'm stupid—because he earned it. Because he stepped in when no one else would.

But it's been too long now. Long enough for doubt to start creeping in again.

Maybe he bailed the second I turned my back. Maybe I was just a distraction, a toy to play with until something shinier came along.

Wouldn't be the first time.

And honestly, I can't even be mad. Not really. He owed me nothing.

Still, there's this irritating voice in my head, scratching at the walls, asking—what if?

What if he stayed? What if he meant it? What if, just this once, someone didn't walk away the second things got complicated?

God, listen to me. This is what happens when adrenaline wears off and the brain tries to turn chaos into connection. When a rescue feels like something more personal. When a deep voice, a big dick, and a little attention short-circuits common sense.

I don't even know him.

But still, some raw, restless part of me wants more. Not some happily-ever-after bullshit.

Just...something that doesn't feel like another warning sign I ignored.

Kayla tugs my hand, snapping me back to the moment, and we move toward the bar, weaving through a pack of drunk men in designer suits. She slams her palm down harder than necessary, demanding the bartender's attention.

"Have you seen our friend?" she yells across the noise. "Blonde, wearing all white, really pretty, a little drunk?"

The bartender barely looks up from mixing. "Babe, that's half the room."

Kayla opens her mouth—probably to tell him exactly where to shove his shaker—but I squeeze her arm.

"Never mind." I run my hand over Kayla's back, hoping to soothe her. "We'll find her."

"Excuse me," a mature voice cuts in. "Did you say white dress?"

I turn to the woman sitting alone at the edge of the bar, sipping something clear with a twist of lime. She looks composed. Polished. The kind of woman who notices things. And remembers.

"Yes," I tell her. "With a white lace mask."

"I saw a girl like that." She leans toward us, as if sharing a secret. "Seemed upset. I think she was crying."

"Please." Kayla steps in, her hands folded under her chin. "Please tell me you saw where she went."

The woman nods, pointing. "She pushed through the crowd maybe twenty minutes ago. I think she told someone she needed air. Slipped out the front door."

A jolt of cold runs through me.

"Thank you." I give her a tight smile and pull Kayla toward the exit.

We push through the noise and velvet and heat, past the faceless bouncer who still gives me the creeps, and step into the damp night. The air's cool, sharp, and a little too clean after the thick press of perfume and sweat inside.

The city stretches out in front of us—from Broadway to the Bronx, lit up and buzzing like it doesn't know or care what we've lost. But there's no sign of Liv. Just endless movement. Strangers brushing past like we don't exist.

Kayla's already got her phone out, hands shaking as she redials, tears cutting tracks down her cheeks. Her voice breaks as she whispers Liv's name into the line again.

I scan the street, searching shadows, alleys, doorways. My pulse hasn't slowed, and my brain's still cycling through worst-case scenarios like it's running code.

Even with panic clawing beneath my skin, he still manages to steal my thoughts.

The stranger in the devil's mask. The filthy mouth. The accidental hero.

I try to focus on what matters. But he lingers—like a ghost in the static—his touch imprinted on my skin. His stare burned into my memory.

It was only ever meant to be one night.

But now he's gone, and I'm still looking back through the door like he might reappear.

Still trying to figure out how the hell I'm supposed to forget him.

Or the way he made me feel.

Chapter 16

Keir

There's no sign of the girl.

I've swept the upstairs—private booths, locked corridors, even the shadowed paths the staff might sneak off to in the middle of a shift. Still nothing.

There are too many distractions. Too much noise. And not one bastard willing to admit they saw something they shouldn't.

I'm down to fuck all. Out of time. Out of luck.

Until one of the servers flags me down. "Hey, I think I saw that blonde you're looking for. She left the floor about twenty minutes ago."

"Anything you can think of that might help me find her?"

She bites the corner of her lip, eyes darting as though checking to see who might be listening. "She was with Bowen Alexander."

My jaw damn near cracks from the pressure.

If it's true, she's gone. And not in the casual, backdoor sort of way. Bowen doesn't do casual. He does silence. His favorite magic trick? Making girls disappear after he's done ruining them.

No mess. No noise. Just a void where something bright used to be.

And now I've got to tell Róisín.

Yeah, I should walk away now. There's nothing more I can do.

I told her one night, and I fucking meant it. There's no way she and I can have anything more. Not when I've lied to her all night. Not with the threat of my uncle breathing down my neck.

But I've already broken every rule I came in with.

I head back down, cutting through the gold-lit room, ignoring the noise, the flesh, the spectacle of it all.

And then I spot her. My sweet little rose.

She's on the far side of the lounge. Moving fast. Mask still on. Clutching her little purse like it's keeping her upright.

She's with the other girl, both heading for the exit. Fast.

I should stop her.

Tell her what I found. Tell her what it means. Give her something more than a filthy fuck and the fallout.

But if I tell her what I know, the lies will crack open. She'll see me for what I am.

A fucking liar.

And if I follow her now… Christ, I won't stop. I'll chase her straight out of this club and into the rest of her goddamn life.

Because she's not just temptation.

She's my fucking downfall in a tight red dress.

So, instead of goodbye, I watch her go.

And order myself another drink.

Chapter 17

Róisín

It's been ten days since Liv disappeared from that fucking club.

Ten days of dead ends and disappearing leads. Of stone-faced cops, slippery club managers, and men in tailored suits who suddenly develop selective amnesia the second The Black Crown is mentioned.

Kayla's still here. She doesn't want to be alone in the apartment she shares with Liv, so she's sleeping on my couch, and making coffee like it's fuel for war.

I can't blame her. Being alone sucks.

Truth is, I like having her around. She's good company, and keeping her close makes it easier to watch her back. We've even fallen into a routine—swinging by their place every day, just in case Liv shows up. We always leave empty-handed, but it hasn't stopped us from trying.

God, how we've tried.

We filed reports. Called every hospital in the five boroughs. Dug through security camera footage we were absolutely not supposed to have. Cornered the staff. Hunted down anyone who might've seen her leave.

We've done everything we're supposed to. Followed all the protocols and all the rules—even as we broke a few.

All we've got to show for it is that one woman from the bar who thinks she saw Liv walk out. *Thinks.* No confirmation. No footage. No solid lead.

Just a ghost in a white dress no one wants to admit ever existed.

And she's not the only one who went missing that night.

The devil vanished too.

Not that I'm shocked. With that veiled accent, and the way he stared at me like he already owned me, plus the real convenient timing when he showed up to play savior, I have a sneaking suspicion disappearing is his specialty.

And if I ever needed to track him down, I'm pretty sure I'd start with Gael O'Shea's crew.

Which is exactly why, no matter how deliciously hot and tempting the memory, I've locked it away with him in the past.

Because I'm still breathing, which is a fucking miracle considering what O'Shea and his men are capable of. Handing over the device only confirmed it. They're brutal. Calculating. Unforgiving. The kind of men who don't give second chances unless they see value in keeping you alive.

I must've been useful enough to earn a sliver of mercy. The data pull worked, I held up my end of the deal, and in return they let me walk. Me and my brother. For now.

But mercy from men like O'Shea always comes with strings. Or an expiration date. So, I'm not wasting time.

What matters now is finding out what happened to Liv. Where she went. If she's still alive.

And I'm done asking nicely.

I sit in the half-dark of my bedroom, laptop open, cursor blinking like it's got something smart to say.

Whoever took her thinks they buried her. That the trail's gone cold.

But they don't know me.

I'm not some drunk girl who danced with the wrong guy and went home crying. I'm not just another outsider who stumbled into their twisted little world.

I'm a hacker.

And I'm going to find her.

Even if I have to rip the city and all its criminals open to do it.

Chapter 18

Keir

Christ, this place reeks. Like sweat-soaked socks, stale beer, and the kind of filth that settles into the bones of a man who's never had to answer for anything.

I wait in the dark, fists clenched, jaw locked tight. This isn't about patience—it's about purpose. Making it count.

When the door finally creaks open, I stay tucked back in the shadows, letting the hallway light stretch across the floor without touching me. No sense spoiling the surprise too soon.

Keys hit the table. A can hisses open. He belches like the pig he is.

Good. Let the bastard get comfortable. Let him think he's safe.

The sound of his unsteady steps grows louder—boots scraping over cheap linoleum. He stumbles into the room, half-pissed already.

"Hello, Bobby." My voice is low. Flat. The calm before a bloody storm.

He startles like a rat in a trap, the beer slipping from his hand and hitting the floor with a dull thud. He goes for the cabinet. For the gun that isn't there.

I let him fumble. Let the panic settle in deep. Watch it hollow him out from the inside.

He finds the drawer empty and turns to me with both hands raised, eyes wide and voice cracking. "Whatever you want—take it."

I laugh. "What makes you think I'd want any of your shite? Honestly, Bobby, your place is a dump."

He lowers his hands an inch, confusion crumpling his face. "I don't—"

"Save it," I cut him off. I don't want his questions. I'm here for fucking answers. "I'm not a thief. Not like you and your pal, Bowen Alexander. How's he these days?"

"Wait, wait, wait," he stammers, his hands shaking violently now. "I've got nothing to do with that asshole."

"Ah, come on now. You and I both know that's not true. You were with him less than two weeks ago at The Black Crown."

His mouth flaps open, but all he can manage is a wheeze. Like it's his dying breath.

Soon enough, you little prick.

"You remember the night," I continue, casual as you like, even as my blood rises. Christ, I'd love to punch him. "You were there, pushing around a gorgeous redhead. I was there, stopping you."

"Fuck, it's you."

I nod once. "Yeah. It's me."

"I didn't mean—fuck, it wasn't my call. Alexander—he was the one—"

"I'm not here about her." My voice hardens. "I'm here about the blonde."

He blinks. "Blonde?"

"Don't fuck with me."

"I thought you were with the redhead."

I move toward him, menace in every step. "Don't mistake where my loyalty lies."

Because he doesn't know. No one fucking knows that every goddamn second since that night has been filled with her.

Róisín. My sweet little rose.

The fire in her voice, the way she looked at me like I was her goddamn salvation. The feel of her body. The lies between us. The truth I'll never get to tell.

She's gone. And I'll never touch her again. Never hear her laugh, or curse, or call me out with that sharp little tongue of hers. I'd tear this whole city apart for one more second with her.

But we'll never have a proper goodbye.

Instead, I get this.

Bobby raises his hands again, this time like he thinks he can reason with me. "I swear, man. I don't know anything. Alexander cut me loose that night. I haven't seen him since."

"No idea where he went? What he did after?"

"None."

Something inside me twists. The last scrap of hope, torn in half and left bleeding.

"That's a pity," I say through a heavy sigh. "Could've saved your pathetic life."

It's a lie, but there's a sick kind of satisfaction in letting him think it's true. Even if only for this moment.

I should draw it out. Beat him senseless. Make him feel every second of the terror he gave her. But a fight brings trouble, and I'm not here for that.

The only thing he can offer me now is closure.

He sees his gun before I raise it. His eyes go wide, mouth moving too fast, voice shrill and useless.

But I don't listen.

I think of Róisín. Her mouth. Her body. The sounds she made as she came apart around me. The silence that followed.

"Tell the devil I send my regards."

And I pull the trigger.

Want more Róisín and Keir? You can pre-order their next book, Tame the Devil now: https://books2read.com/tamethedevil

. . .

Or signup to receive email updates about the release: https://kimberlyquinn.myflodesk.com/bjux0059ag

Also by Kimberly Quinn

DARK ROMANCES:

Savage Hearts Empire Series

Tempt the Devil

Tame the Devil

more to come...

Savage Hearts Syndicate Series

Sweet Chaos

Lovely Torment (releasing Nov. 18, 2025)

Pretty Ruin (releasing May 2026)

Beautiful Trouble (releasing Nov. 2026)

SMALL TOWN ROMANCES:

Stirling Bay Series

Complex Kisses

Fairytale Kisses

Illicit Kisses

Standalone

Love on the Rocks

Canyon Spring Series

(in collaboration with S.M. West)

The Cowboy Bargain

The Cowboy Hitch

more to come...

Acknowledgments

Thanks to my editors, The Happily Editing Anns, for the excellent work and endless patience with my delays. You're both amazing!

Rebecca, you don't just keep my social media looking great, you show up with the enthusiasm and energy I need to get through the day. Thank you.

To the readers who've shown up for me time and again: the biggest thank you from the depths of my dark little heart.

Sarah, you're a hero for putting up with my rants, and for always being in my corner. Life wouldn't be the same without you.

Sybil, you've been an endless source of support, inspiration, and knowledge. I'm so thankful to call you my friend.

About the Author

Kimberly is a contemporary romance author, born procrastinator, and lover of morally gray heroes. She enjoys lively conversations, usually with imaginary people, and can often be found daydreaming at work.

She writes gritty, messy, and sometimes dangerous romances, featuring beautifully flawed characters, pursuing love at all costs. It's romance with rough edges.

When she's not busy writing, you can find her with a coffee in hand, dog at her side, and exploring the wilds of her hometown in Ontario, Canada... Or on her couch, getting lost in a good story.

www.kimberlyquinnbooks.com

instagram.com/kimberlyquinn.books
facebook.com/kimberlyquinnbooks
bookbub.com/profile/kimberly-quinn
amazon.com/stores/Kimberly-Quinn/author/B0BV18S35M

Manufactured by Amazon.ca
Bolton, ON

55920181R00062